Where Did It Go?

Dog put water in a cup on Monday.
Dog put the cup in the freezer.

2

On Tuesday, the water was gone.
There was ice in the cup.
Where did the water go?

3

Cat put the ice in his wagon on Tuesday.
He put his wagon in the sun.

On Wednesday, the ice was gone.
There was water in the wagon.
Where did the ice go?

Dog put the cup in water on Wednesday.

Dog put the wet cup in the sun.

On Thursday, the water on the cup was gone.
The cup was dry.
Where did the water go?

Cat put water in the cup on Thursday.
Cat put sugar in the water.

8

On Friday, the sugar was gone.
The water tasted sweet.
Where did the sugar go?

9

Cat put water in the cup on Friday.
Cat put a lollipop in the water.

On Saturday, the lollipop was gone.
The water was pink.
Where did the lollipop go?

Cat looked at the pink water in the cup on Saturday.
Cat put more lollipops in the water.

On Sunday, the lollipops were gone.
The water was red.
Where did the lollipops go?

Dog put some cookies in the cookie jar on Sunday morning.

On Sunday night, the cookies were gone.
Where did the cookies go?

15

Cat knows!